The Whistling Tree

by Audrey Penn

Illustrated by Barbara Leonard Gibson

Child & Family Press

Washington, DC

Child & Family Press is an imprint of the Child Welfare League of America. The Child Welfare League of America is the nation's oldest and largest membership-based child welfare organization. We are committed to engaging people everywhere in promoting the well-being of children, youth, and their families, and protecting every child from harm.

© 2003 by Audrey Penn. All rights reserved. Neither this book nor any part may be reproduced or transmitted in any form or by any means, electronic or mechanical, including photocopying, microfilming, and recording, or by any information storage and retrieval system, without permission in writing from the publisher. For information on this or other CWLA publications, contact the CWLA Publications Department at the address below.

CHILD WELFARE LEAGUE OF AMERICA, INC., HEADQUARTERS

440 First Street NW, Third Floor

Washington, DC 20001-2085

www.cwla.org

E-mail: books@cwla.org

CURRENT PRINTING (last digit)

10 9 8 7 6 5 4 3 2 1

Printed in the United States of America

Cover and text design by James D. Melvin

Edited by Tegan A. Culler

ISBN # 0–87868–852–8

Library of Congress Cataloging-in-Publication Data

Penn, Audrey, 1947-

  The whistling tree / by Audrey Penn ; illustrated by Barbara Leonard Gibson.

     p. cm.

Summary: When Penny begins searching for the source of the mysterious whistling she hears in her sleep, her parents take her to meet her great-great-uncle, who tells her about her Cherokee heritage.

  ISBN 0-87868-852-8 (alk. paper)

  1. Cherokee Indians--Juvenile fiction. [1. Cherokee Indians--Fiction.

2. Indians of North America--North Carolina--Juvenile fiction. 3. North Carolina--Fiction.] I. Gibson, Barbara, ill. II. Title.

  PZ7.P38448Wh 2003

  [E]--dc21

            2002155214

In honor of Louise, John, Joan, Joel, and Valery,
their children,
and their proud Cherokee heritage.
And to my friend Pierre, who hugs trees.

enny was six years old the first time she heard the whistling. It came to her in a dream and whisked her away on a ribbon of melody. Sometimes the whistling was soft and low. Other times, it was shrill and twittering. Then came the harmony: A chorus of whistling like the lyrical tones of a thousand flutes. Weeks and months and years flew by, and Penny danced in her dreams, swirling and turning until the morning sun quieted the music and gently woke her to a new day.

Then there were the lights. Blues and purples, greens and whites. Tiny pinlights, like the tip of a sparkler, flickered in front of Penny's sleeping eyes.

One night, the deep, airy tones of a wooden flute floated through Penny's dreams and stirred her awake. Penny slipped out of bed and followed the sound into the hallway and up toward the ceiling. As her eyes rested on the attic door, the fluting stopped.

Nights and weeks and months passed, and the sweet sound of flutes and whistles stayed silent. The dancing lights dimmed. One day, Penny stood beneath the attic door and stared at the pull chain. Her heart pounded and her tiny hands trembled. She had never climbed into the attic. It was the room where memories lived. But she missed the whistling and the lights, so she gripped the chain, pulled down the old maplewood ladder, and climbed upward, one terrifying step at a time.

Silence stood among the old things, but the sun streamed in through the attic window and calmed Penny's fears. Closing her eyes, she eagerly awaited the melodic flutes and fairy-dust lights.

Soon, a single note whispered in her ear. Then a second. Then another, until a symphony of whistles and a spattering of colorful lights hummed and danced in Penny's head.

Penny laughed and twirled atop the attic planks. She opened her eyes and followed the whistling to an old bed quilt leaning against the back wall. She touched the quilt and it slipped to the floor, revealing a wooden headboard.

Penny gently traced the graceful, hand-carved design with the tip of her finger. An orchestration of whistles and flutes rose from the pine-scented headboard up into the rafters, then once again grew silent. It was time to go back down.

"Where did the headboard in the attic come from?" Penny asked her mother.

"My grandfather, your great-grandfather, hand carved that headboard when he was just a boy. He gave it to my father, and my father passed it on to me. Would you like to have it in your bedroom?"

Penny exploded with joy. "Oh, yes. Thank you!" she said, jumping and spinning about the kitchen. "Please, may I have it now?"

Penny's parents were delighted, and the headboard was brought to her room.

That night, the song of distant flutes and soft-sounding whistles feathered Penny's dreams, filling her head with melodious whirlwinds and tender harmonies. Lights twinkled and burst in vibrant reds, dandelion yellows, firelight ambers, and stormy grays. And there was more: Rich, savory images of sunlit meadows, thick forests, and rushing rivers.

"Where did my great-grandfather find the wood and make the headboard?" Penny asked her mother.

"Would you like to see for yourself?" Penny's mother asked her.

"Oh yes, thank you!" said Penny, bouncing and clapping with delight. "Please, can we go right away?"

Penny's family arrived at Woodpecker Hollow just as the sun set. The North Carolina mountains were steep and winding, and the western sky blushed in shy, pastel pinks and radiant oranges. Penny stepped out of the car and stared at an ancient log cabin pressed against a background of open fields and newly built houses. In the distance, a single crop of century-old trees stood proud and regal among a new generation of saplings.

Penny and her parents walked up the sidewalk just as the cabin door swung open. An old man dressed in blue jeans and a fringed shirt hurried toward them with his hands held out in greeting. His skin was thick and tanned and wrinkled, like the cracks in dried clay, and a long, gray ponytail cascaded down his back. Penny stared at the colorful beaded belt circling the man's waist. Each bead sparkled like a single shining pinlight from her dreams. A large silver buckle in the shape of a soaring eagle proudly adorned the center.

"This is your great-great-uncle, Johnny Elk," Penny's mother told her. "He was my grandfather's youngest brother."

"Are you an Indian?" asked Penny.

Johnny Elk grinned so wide, Penny was afraid a piece of his dry, crinkly face would chip off. "I am a son of the Cherokee Nation," he said proudly. "You and your mother are also Cherokee Indians. Like the leaves of a tree, we are nourished from the same roots. Your mother tells me you have my brother's headboard. I am grateful that you are giving it new life." Johnny Elk led Penny and her parents into the house and pointed to a photograph hanging on the living room wall. "This is a picture of my brother when he was a child. He lived on a small reservation not far from here. He hand carved your headboard out of a tree that had fallen in a storm."

Johnny Elk showed Penny and her parents the rest of his log cabin and invited them to make themselves at home. Penny's father studied the many pictures that hung throughout the house. Penny's mother examined the hand-carved furnishings and colorful pieces of pottery that had been handed down through twelve generations of Cherokee relatives.

"How did you get your name?" Penny asked Johnny Elk.

"Cherokee names are not always given at birth," explained her uncle. "We, like you and your friends, are often given English names. But sometimes, after you have done something special, a Cherokee name is given. I was eleven years old when I received the name Johnny Elk. I was on a camping trip in Canada with my father and two of my uncles. One night, I heard a commotion and peeked out of my bedroll to see what was going on. A baby elk had come into our camp and was eating our food.

"The next day, I kept watch over our things while my father and uncles went out hunting. My father had warned me to watch out for the baby elk's mother. If she caught me near her calf, she would come after me.

"While I was at the campsite alone, the little elk's mother came to fetch her calf. I was too scared to run or yell for help, so I climbed up a tree and watched the elk from there. My father and uncles laughed at me later for being a coward. Instead of chasing away the elk, I watched as they gobbled up our food!"

That night, Penny dreamt the story of Johnny Elk and laughed in her sleep.

Early the next morning, Penny and her uncle walked across clover meadows and grassy fields toward the grove of age-old trees.

"When your great-grandfather was a young boy, most of these hills were forest. That grove is all that is left. This stream that we are following was once a powerful river. Birds and animals lived here in abundance, and freshwater fish danced on the ends of our fishing lines."

Penny's eyes were drawn to the trees. Her tiny fingers ached to touch their thick, ancient bark. The dance of flickering fire lit her insides as she stepped ceremoniously onto the small plot of ground that honored the last remaining Tall Pines.

"They're beautiful," she told her uncle as she danced around the trees and hugged them one by one.

"Yes, they are," said Johnny Elk. "But this is all that is left of Woodpecker Hollow."

Penny sat down on a giant boulder and watched the stream skip and gurgle over tree roots and rocks.

"Why is this place called Woodpecker Hollow?" she asked her uncle.

Johnny Elk smiled at the memory.

"Over one hundred years ago, when birds nested here and animals roamed freely, there was a bitter argument between the songbirds and a woodpecker. It is told that in early spring, while the snow still covered the woods like a goose-down quilt, songbirds built their nests and laid their eggs. Animals, too, gave birth to their young, and fish spawned.

"Each spring, the woodpecker also returned to the forest. He would fly to the tallest trees in the woods and begin his rat-a-tat-tatting. He would rat-a-tat-tat all morning, and rat-a-tat-tat all day. He would stay on one tree until several large limbs were covered in woodpecker holes, then move on to another tree.

"The woodpecker made so much noise, the songbirds couldn't sing, and their babies couldn't sleep. Animals complained and schools of fish deserted the river.

"Finally, all of the birds, animals, and remaining fish complained to the woodpecker that he must stop his rat-a-tat-tatting at once and give them some peace."

"Well," said her uncle, "that did not go over well with the woodpecker. He grew bolder and bolder and his rat-a-tat-tatting grew louder and louder.

"Eventually, the songbirds gave up their singing. Their babies fell from their nests exhausted. Animals grew tired and limp. And the last of the fish left forever.

"The woodpecker finally understood, and the following spring, he did not return to the woods. This made the birds and animals very happy, and life was good in the forest.

"Then one day, there came a terrible wind. Tree limbs shattered, and nests tumbled from the trees. Baby animals stumbled to the ground, helpless and crying. The songbirds were about to give up all hope when a heavenly sound flew out of the tops of the trees and spread across the swirling sky."

"Whistling!" exclaimed Penny. She looked over at her uncle to find him staring straight at her, nodding his head and smiling.

"You can hear it, can't you, Penny?"

"I really can," said Penny, nodding back. "It's light and airy some of the time. And sometimes it's like a thousand flutes, all playing at once."

"It's the sound the trees made when the wind ribboned in and out of the woodpecker holes," explained her uncle. "The whistling lifted their spirits and gave the birds and animals courage to survive the windstorm. After that, the woodpecker was welcomed wherever he went."

"Only a few people have ever heard the whistling trees," Johnny Elk told Penny. "Your great-grandfather heard it and made his headboard out of one of the trees the woodpecker had drilled. He was a medicine man, your great-grandfather. A healer. Perhaps you too are a healer, for you too can hear the whistling. I shall call you Penny Who Hears the Trees."

"Uncle?" asked Penny. "What about the lights?"

Johnny Elk regarded his grandniece joyfully. "Then you do see lights. I hoped you could."

The elder Cherokee beheld Penny's long, chestnut hair and shy Indian features. "The moment we are born, both our spirit and a single bright star come alive within us. Our spirit ties us to things here on earth, such as the trees and rivers and other people. The star ties us to things outside of ourselves, like the sun and the moon and the galaxies.

"While our spirit stays within us both day and night, our star shines like the sun and sends out rays during the day. These rays soar out of our bodies, into the sky, and out among the heavens. At night, the rays return to us, bringing with them a sprinkling of stars that only a few chosen people can see. You, child, are one of the chosen few. The Great Spirit has chosen you to see the lights and hear the whistling trees."

Johnny Elk reached out and took Penny Who Hears the Trees by the hand. "Come, child. It is time to leave Woodpecker Hollow."

Penny gave each tree a loving hug and thanked them for their gifts of music and harmony. She also thanked her great-great-uncle for his stories and wisdom, and she promised to return to Woodpecker Hollow.

In the car going home, Penny held the feathered and beaded dreamcatcher her great-great-uncle had made for her. That night, when she was safely tucked into bed, her gentle hands brushed against her great-grandfather's wooden headboard. Borrowed memories from a forest long ago played an aria of flutes and whistles in her head. Tiny pinlights, like the tip of a sparkler, twinkled across her closed, sleeping eyes. Penny could hear the colorful tones of a forest of whistling trees for nights, and weeks, and months, and forever.